For Oghenebrume Naomi Anigboro —N. G.

For Nikki —W. M.

BLOOMSBURY CHILDREN'S BOOKS
Bloomsbury Publishing Inc., part of Bloomsbury Publishing Plc
1385 Broadway, New York, NY 10018

BLOOMSBURY, BLOOMSBURY CHILDREN'S BOOKS, and the Diana logo are trademarks of Bloomsbury Publishing Plc

First published in the United States of America in May 2020
by Bloomsbury Children's Books

Bloomsbury books may be purchased for business or promotional use. For information on bulk purchases
please contact Macmillan Corporate and Premium Sales Department at specialmarkets@macmillan.com

Library of Congress Cataloging-in-Publication Data
Names: Grimes, Nikki, author. | Minor, Wendell, illustrator.
Title: Southwest sunrise / by Nikki Grimes ; illustrated by Wendell Minor.
Description: [New York] : Bloomsbury Children's Books, 2020.
Summary: Jayden expects to see nothing but brown his first morning in New Mexico,
but after being surprised by colorful rocks, flowers, birds, and animals,
he wonders if this place could become home.
Identifiers: LCCN 2019044637
ISBN 978-1-5476-0082-3 (hardcover) • ISBN 978-1-5476-0083-0 (e-book) • ISBN 978-1-5476-0084-7 (e-PDF)
Subjects: CYAC: Moving, Household—Fiction. | Nature—Fiction. | Color—Fiction. |
African Americans—Fiction. | New Mexico—Fiction.
Classification: LCC PZ7.G88429 Sou 2020 | DDC [E]—dc23
LC record available at https://lccn.loc.gov/2019044637

Art created with gouache watercolor on Strathmore 500 Bristol Paper
Typeset in Mrs Eaves • Book design by John Candell
Printed in China by Leo Paper Products, Heshan, Guangdong
2 4 6 8 10 9 7 5 3 1

All papers used by Bloomsbury Publishing Plc are natural, recyclable products made from wood grown in well-managed forests.
The manufacturing processes conform to the environmental regulations of the country of origin.

To find out more about our authors and books visit www.bloomsbury.com and sign up for our newsletters.

SOUTHWEST SUNRISE

Nikki Grimes

Children's Literature Legacy Award winner

illustrated by **Wendell Minor**

BLOOMSBURY
CHILDREN'S BOOKS
NEW YORK LONDON OXFORD NEW DELHI SYDNEY

Too old to cry myself to sleep,
I hide behind my baseball cap,
close my eyes, and pout
all the way from New York
to New Mexico,
mad about moving to a place
of shadows.
That's all I see when we land.

Why are we here?
What's so great about
New Mexico?

I wake up to
a knife of sunlight
slicing through the room
Dad says is mine.
I rub my eyes,
stare out the barless window
at a mountain
striped in rainbow.
Hey! Who put that there?
I didn't see it last night.

I pad across a cool tile floor,
spy a rope of red chili peppers
dangling in the kitchen window.
Bet it's the only color I'll find here.
Everybody knows
browns and tans
are the only colors
deserts are good for.

Even so, I step outside
to take a look around,
gripping the field guide
Mom gave me at breakfast.
I flip through the pages,
spot fancy-named flowers
in lots of bright shades
I don't expect to find.

Wait! There's the one
called wine-cup
spilling its burgundy beauty
for me to drink up.

And aren't those yellow bells?
They wake up the desert
with their silent ring.

I look up,
try to understand
the deep waves of turquoise
overhead.
I search for the end of blue,
but there is none.
Where was all this sky
in New York City?
Was it hiding?

Never mind the sky.
I still miss the feeling of wow
craning my neck to study
the tops of skyscrapers.

I lower my eyes
to watch where I'm going.
A giant black bird parades by,
feathers slick as wet hair.
I cluck at him
like he's a simple city crow,
but the guidebook says
he's a raven.
The kingly bird
cocks his proud head and
stares me down for the insult,
then slowly struts away,
certain I can't catch him.

My early morning walk
kicks up another surprise:
one stunned cousin
of the alligator.
I squat down,
catch the lizard
with cupped hands,
feel his curved digits skitter
along my palm,
as ready to run
as I am to let him.

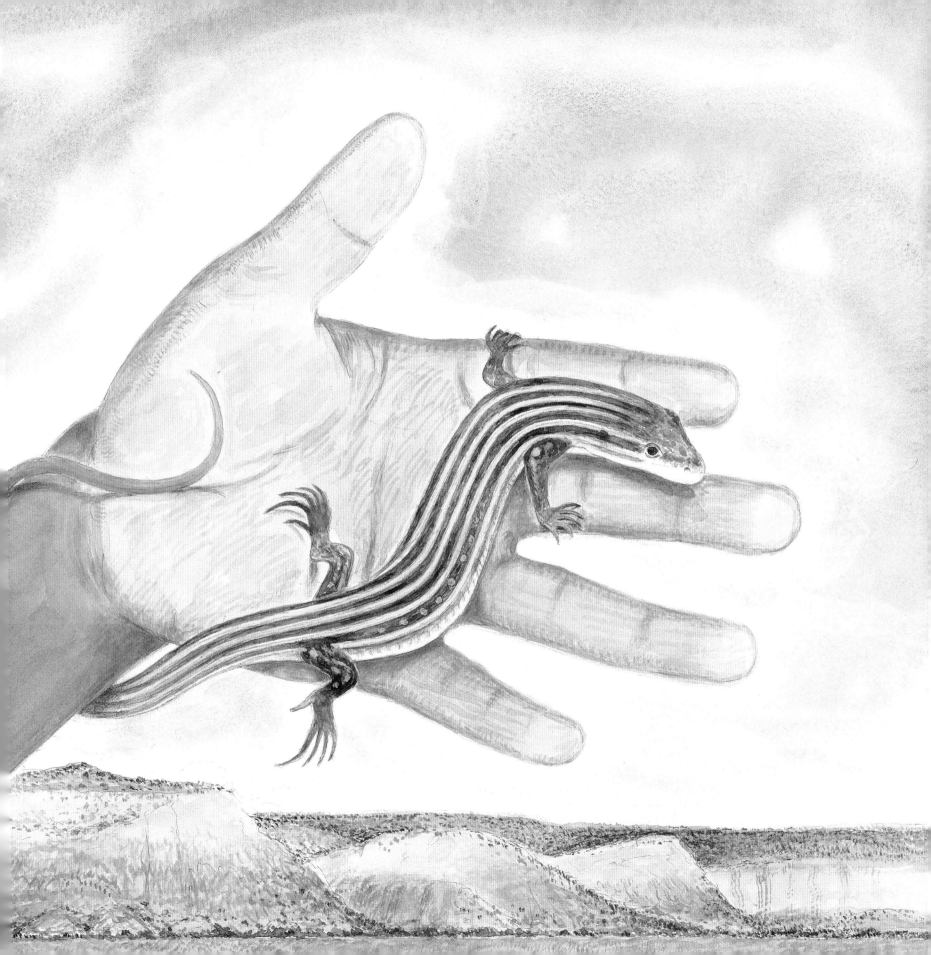

I shiver from the silence
unbroken by
the familiar sound of sirens—
but not for long.
A few yards down the road,
I pick up the mad chatter
of winged gossips
passing secrets
from one unfamiliar tree to another.
The guidebook calls them
piñon trees.

Oh! Hot red firewheel flowers!
Their tips flame yellow-orange
across the canyon.

There's a patch of calypso orchids!
So glad I didn't miss them
dancing purple in the wind.
My mom will love those.

What do you know?
Opposite our house
I discover
another kind of color,
a house made of pinkish clay
with edges round as bubbles.
Adobe.

Someone should tell these
flying chatterboxes
magpies are beautiful
when their beaks are still,
when they sail on air
and write across the sky
with the long black tips
of their tails.

I shade my eyes
from the desert sun
and squint.
The river of sand
washes up bleached bones
like seashells
at Jones Beach:
rib, bird's skull, turtle shell.
What stories
do they have to tell?

I reach road's end,
turn the corner,
and am startled by
stone towers off in the distance:
red rock pillars
holding up the sky.
Daddy should've told me
this new place has
its own skyscrapers!

"Jayden!"
I hear Mom's voice
cut through the quiet.
Time to head back,
but not before I pick
a few flowers.

I wave to Mom
where she waits
on the porch,
flash her
a fistful of flowers,
and the first smile she's seen
since New York.
Maybe I can think about
calling this place Home.